Stand-Up Summer

Summer

Dr. Leslie Sutter

outskirtspress
DENVER, COLORADO

Outskirts Press, Inc.
http://www.outskirtspress.com

ISBN: 978-1-4327-9138-4

Outskirts Press and the "OP" logo are trademarks belonging to Outskirts Press, Inc.

PRINTED IN THE UNITED STATES OF AMERICA

To
All those who stand up and make us laugh at
ourselves and our world

Table of Contents

1 Why? 1

2 Time to Stand-up................................... 7

3 Getting Ready 25

4 On the Mic: the Basics......................... 29

5 The Road and Bombs Away in the West 38

6 After Bombing a Roast 51

7 Good Advice for the Road...................... 57

8 Scouted... 66

9 TV Taping.. 74

10 Stand-up or Fall.................................. 79

Intro

This is a work of fiction and does not attempt to document the world of stand-up comedy.

If you are interested in that area I would direct you to three good DVDs: I Am Comic (2010), Heckler (2008) and When Stand Up Stood Out (2005).

I have used sources and material from real comedians, books, DVDs and websites which I have rewritten, adopted and revised to add authenticity, and as these sources all say the same thing in a different way, I apologize if I step on anyone's toes by misquoting the general rules-of-the-road. I list my favorite sources at the end of this novel and thank them now for their valuable input.

If you wish to try your hand at stand up, the basics are built into the storyline. All you have to do is find a club near you with an open mic evening. There are countless stories of going from an unknown to stardom in nothing flat (just read an internet biography on your favorite comic) so the plot is not far from reality. Enjoy.

1
Why?

I want to tell the story of my stand-up summer for two reasons: first to encourage readers to take a chance on their dreams, or conversely to scare them off from doing so. Either way I hope to make a small difference. I also, somehow, need to get it all out of my mind, off my chest and putting it down on paper seems to be the best way because I don't want to forget the long road I took with Franky that summer.

So here I sit, exhausted and exhilarated in a dark comedy club after closing on a Wednesday night open microphone. If this were a movie the establishing shot would be of Firerock Community College in glorious Centerville. I won't say which state because this boring town could be almost anywhere. Cut to a wide shot of the red brick 2-story campus buildings, slowly narrowing in a slow zoom to an old man, walking alone, muttering to long-dead associates about forgotten events. The monotone self-talk usually revolves around how he (the college president) upgraded the institution from a vocational cooking school for juvenile delinquents to what it is today, a community college for juvenile delinquents.

The patriarch of Firerock, Dr. (honorary) Ned Stroller obtained employment here around thirty years ago by somehow being related to Gerald Firerock, who invented a carburetor no longer in use. Anyway, Firerock founded the place with cash and farmland.

"Dr." Stroller, as he insists being addressed, is on the way to a ceremony granting tenure to three professors. The first is myself, Dr. Michael Stanthrop (English), my best friend Professor Frank Ledbetter, M.A. (Philosophy) and my best girl and love of my life, Dr. Karen Smith (Speech).

We have waited a long five years to finally reach this academic milestone and get "bulletproof." It means getting 'the suits' off your back for good. It means you can snap at snotty little punk students. It means you can shoot up heroin in front of a class and pack a machine gun. Well, almost. It is major job security and getting rarer at institutions of higher learning.

No one was more pleased at making the grade than Franky. Barely completing his alternative master's degree, he never even started a Ph.D. program and intends to coast the rest of his career. He is, as is often said of him, a screw-up and wears that title like a badge of honor. Being a philosophy professor entitles him to openly anti-authoritarian activity and disguises his confused mental state behind the rouge of the Socratic method.

Professor Franky is always in trouble for some reason, but he made tenure because the "trouble" was always unrelated to his job performance: he was advisor to the GLBT (i.e. Gay Lesbian Bi Transgender) club which sponsored a popular cross-dressing day on campus to the horror of the Board of Trustees and Dr. Stroller; he took his ethics classes on a field trip to the pet cemetery and openly mocked mourners; he circulated petitions for a nude beach in Centerville (there is no beach). He also raised a considerable amount of money for the student union with his annual foreign film festival, in which he purposely chose the weirdest and most incomprehensible films no one really understood, least of all the people who made them.

My favorite was the Mongolian/Albanian co-production of a Yiddish-dubbed and Urdu-subtitled animated 3d safe-sex documentary: "Yak in the Yurt." Intellectuals pretended to comprehend its subtler points while the students and artists raved about its powerful, liberating message. Actually, Franky just mixed up the part I and part II cassettes and played it backwards.

Franky has some tics. One is that he deludedly believes that women way above his league are eyeing him (or us) in public places. The scenario that usually unfolds on "boy's night out" is a Dutch-treat which rapidly turns into an I-forgot-my-wallet, I'm a bit short, I forgot to my credit/debit/ATM card. I always get the money back, so I don't know why he always does this. He insists on a corner table with his back to the wall and an escape route because he believes it turns women on by demonstrating 'gangster aura.' It usually means you can smell and hear the kitchen staff. Next he will ask the waiter if everything is fresh. I am still waiting for a smart aleck waiter to say no, sir, not fresh, only rotten, almost inedible ingredients! Why even ask? After annoying the waiter, he will signal me.

"Mike, the hot blondes at the table behind you are shooting us looks!"

"Of course they are, you sucker-punched them with your gangsta yin yang ding dong."

"Mike! I am making serious eye contact. They want us. I will now send a hypno-magnetic stare to draw them in." He glared at them.

"Ok, Houdini-Spengali, mesmerize them babes, reel them in." I toyed with my blue cheese stuffed olive and sipped my dirty martini awaiting the inevitable.

"Wait, oh cancel that order. Deal breaker!"

"What did the bad girl do?" I asked vaguely bored.

"Not with me! Her hoop earrings are not of the appropriate size."

"Damn! I missed that, thanks for having standards." Actually they were freakishly huge.

"I know," he groaned, "if you let that slide, it is domino city, slippery slope, last straw on the camel toe…"

"Uh, I think it was the camel's back…mmmm." I looked at the specials. The vodka peanut-butter tuna-Asian-fusion sliders looked good.

"Snowball! Avalanche, gateway drug, blockbuster, there goes the neighborhood!" he babbled on, loud enough for everyone to hear.

No wonder he's still single.

But back to the tenure ceremony. As "Dr." Stroller bleated on and on, I was highly on edge because my fiancée, Karen, was acting very distant. I will admit that the strain of teaching full-time and both of us finishing up our dissertations had taken a lot of the romance out of our relationship; however I was convinced that we could get back on track this summer, starting right after this ceremony, with the help of a bottle of fine champagne.

I was wrong.

Note to self: whenever a woman says 'we have to talk' it isn't good. I thought she wanted to set a firm wedding date but she wanted to spend the summer 'as just friends' and 'get some perspective about life.'

I was dumped.

2
Time to Stand-up

I won't lie and say the break-up was easy. Even though she tried to make it seem mutual, it wasn't: she dumped me. To make it worse, she didn't leave me for another guy, or even a set of hot lesbian twins. She wasn't even dating or looking online. Karen had dumped me for being ME. Instead of living happily-ever-after as the darling couple of Firerock Community College, we were constantly in each other's face on that small campus and every little jerk student knew we were no longer an item. I was depressed and dis-tressed. I couldn't even stalk her; she was right there all the time!

Luckily, Franky had a plan to cheer me up. He tracked me down at the campus supply center. I was stealing photocopy paper for my home computer.

"Mike, tonight we are going out to Club Rainbow in Cedertown!"

I frowned. "Club Rainbow? Franky, turning gay won't help. Bad plan." I also took a dozen red pens. And some glue sticks.

"No, tonight is Wednesday, a slow night for the club so they do an open comedy show. No cover and a discounted two drink minimum! Amateur comics do their routines. It will cheer you up, bro. I'll drive. We'll take your car. Spot me a little cash and we're good to go. If it blows we'll drink up and depart." He purloined three dry erase markers and a tiny pocket stapler.

"What the hell," I said zipping closed my loaded backpack.

"Opa!" He twirled in a little Greek dance and pocketed some paper clips.

So began my first exposure to live stand-up.

To offer some background, "Comedy Open Mic" is a crucial part of being a comedian when you are first starting out. I place it in the same category as a porn star going to a shoot, not bothering to stretch. Someone or something is going to get bent, and in a comic's case, it will be their routine and their pride.

If you are at the point where you are a successful comedian, and you have never had to do dozens of free open mic performances, please let me know your secret. Basically, it is impossible!

I'm being facetious, because I know some comics out there that have never had to do unpaid open mic. They are rare as Bigfoot. I could only wish I were so good that I got paid from the start, but I fell in with the 99% that started out on open mic. But hey, look on the bright side; the pay is usually so ridiculously low in the minor leagues, there isn't much difference. Too many call the backseat of their car "the Hilton" aka where they will sleep most nights on the road.

Again, if you are new to doing stand-up then comedy open mic is essential. It not only is a place for you to practice new material after you get sick of the bathroom mirror, but it is also a great place to make connections with other comics in your area and even in your state or country. I say that because if you are serious about being a comic, you will travel around the country like I did, stopping at every hick town to deliver a five minute monologue in every kind of weather.

Comedy open mics are a marketing stunt by the owner of the "comedy club," which is often primarily a bar and restaurant most of the week. They do not have to open the stage up for any of us; to them I say thank you and you should too--every chance you get. The only benefit to a comedy club may be to see where they can sell a few drinks and find talent for a weekend show.

We took our seats and were slammed with the two-drink minimum. Showtime!

"Our first monologue tonight is from the incredible Mr. Jeremy Alvarez!"

A well-dressed man walked up to the microphone like he had done so many times, and just laid out his routine. I was all ears.

"I have had all sorts of problems lately. I lost my job. My dog ran away. The taxes are always there. My car broke down. I got a terrible rash that I'd prefer not to talk about right now. Oh, and my bathtub randomly exploded. EXPLODED. Don't ask. I don't even know. I mean seriously! I'm not trying to question the universe or anything, but that kind of stuff just plain doesn't happen! It definitely ruined my day. And don't even get me started on the crap that's on daytime television nowadays.

"It's like the entire world is against me. Like I'm just a fictional character for some twisted writer to vent his anger on to make himself feel better about his own life. I know it sounds ridiculous but that's the only thing I can compare it to.

"You know what? I'm being selfish. I've just been telling you all about my problems. I never listen to what you have to say. How's life? (Long pause, laughter)

"Hey, wait just a second here. Something's wrong. (Looks around) What the hell....? I'm not talking to anybody! I've been talking to myself this whole time!

"Am I crazy? Now that I think about it, I don't even remember getting here. (Thinks hard) I can't remember anything before me saying 'I have had all sorts of problems lately.'

"I can't remember any of my life! It's like my life started with that sentence and there was nothing before it!

"Ok, ok, ok, pal, don't panic. There's got to be some reasonable explanation, right? Let's see. Where am I? I'm in some sort of.....room. Alright, that's a start. My god, why do I feel so comfortable talking to myself? Wait. There are people. They're just sitting there.....watching me...???!!!"

"They (gasp) must be some kind of alien race that abducted me and fed me a drug that made me forget my entire life—made me start talking to myself like some kind of mental patient!

He paced the stage like a crazed, caged animal.

"Hey! Aliens! Can you hear me! I'm on to you! I know what you're doing! You want me to freak out until I give up the name and location of the President so you can control his mind and have all of mankind at your command! Well, guess what alien scum! When you brainwashed me, you made me forget everything about the President too! Boy, did you guys screw up! Not so advanced now are ya? Are ya?!?! You guys got yourself into some deep crap this time! Emperor Farquexitonimolaguniasiumtron isn't going to be too happy about that is he?!

"Wait. They don't LOOK like aliens. Hmm. Maybe I jumped the gun a little there. Maybe they'll respond if I ask them what's going on (seeks a victim in the audience).

"Hey! You! Yes, you! Where am I and how did I get here? Stop just staring at me like that! Answer my question! Why are you just watching? Do you want me to do a trick or something? You're staring at me like you're a patron in an audience!

"Wait (long pause). These people...this room... those lights....that hairstyle.... I know what this is! I know where I am! This IS an audience! My greatest fear has finally come true... I'M TRAPPED IN A MONOLOGUE (goes to his knees, throws hands into the air)!!

"Noooooooooooo!!!" Long silence, giggles.

"If this is a monologue, and I have no doubt in my mind that it is, that means that it's only a matter of time! Once the actor says "scene," it's all over for me! I may only have seconds to live. Okay, calm down. I just have to convince him not to say it! Yeah! I'm sure I'm being played by a decent guy. He'll understand.

"Ahem. Uh, hey, Actor! Whatever you do, do not say the word 'scene!' I'm begging you! If you say that word, it's all over for me! Oh, jeez is he even listening to me? Hey, you're a good guy, right? We're on the same team here! If you have any decency at all, you will not say that word! Please!

"Oh, no. I feel myself fading away! That can only mean one thing! He's about to break character! The scene's almost over! Come on, man, think about what you're doing! You can't just bring someone to life just to make them blink out of existence in a time span of a few minutes! What kind of example would you be setting for your peers?!"

(Gets on his knees and starts to grovel) Please, please, please, PLEASE!! Do not say----SCENE!"

Several people in the audience, obviously his friends yell, "SCENE!"

Applause.

Most comics at an open mic will be happy to party-hearty with you and offer advice, sex and drugs in liberal doses. A wild crowd becomes a great family unit once you are accepted, but if you are a stuck-up jackass, you will get the freeze.

You may be a better comedian than others in the room, but if you decide to make sure that everyone else is reminded of it, your place in that family will soon be occupied by another. Word gets around quickly in the internet age. This can be a good thing if you are a good guy.

You may ask, how often should I do a comedy open mic?

I personally say a minimum of once a week you need to be on a stage. That could be a gig or an open mic. Any less than that and you will never be able to stay sharp enough to move forward.

Back to the show. A Chinese girl took the stage.

"Please a warm welcome for our next comic, Xiaoqi Li!!!"

"You know, everyone nowadays has a cell phone. It's like their lives orbit around that rectangular piece of steel...and it's not even a sphere! I can't disagree though...I'm one of those people that just can't part with their phone.

"Every few minutes I'll be checking my phone. Oh look! I have...zero missed calls, zero new texts, the Facebook frontier is quiet...

Then I remember I've had zero incoming calls, zero texts, and I have three friends on Facebook: Mom, Dad, and Grandma. I used to have four but then Grandpa died.

"Anyways, I'll still be sitting there, or standing there, no difference, with my phone, just messing around with it. I have one of those sliding phones... (Towards audience) how many of you guys have those sliding phones? Well, you guys know how addicting it is to just slide the phone back and forth? Click, clack, click, clack.

"It's lots of fun until suddenly, I get a call from my mom wondering why I called. Hello? Oh hi, Mom.... no I didn't mean to call you…no I'm not at a bar right now…yes, I know I don't have a boyfriend…no need to rub it in…no! Do not set me up with someone! Um, I really have to go um…make dinner. Yes, at two am! Love you (shakes head mouthing 'not really'). Bye!

"Later on, I'm going to bed…getting real sleepy… ALERT ALERT. ALERT ALERT

I jumped out of bed, wide awake, grab the pink BB gun I always keep by me in case my feelings get hurt or something...you know.

"I'm going around corners like they do in the movies, looking all cool like Charlie's Angels, the Chinese one of course... in my dinosaur jammies. I get to the room where I still hear ALERT ALERT. ALERT ALERT! going off…and I realize it was my phone.

Nothing like a text alert full volume at three in the morning to get the blood flowing!

"Someone actually texted me! It was…my mom.

"Let's see…I read my mom's message first. It says that Grandma died. Dammit! Now I only have two friends on Facebook. Thank you."

As we applauded, I thought how exciting it would be to be up there, performing live!

I was hooked on the playful fun of stand-up comedy, and for the first time since the break-up I really forgot about myself and my problems and laughed out loud. I also felt the tension of being onstage even though I was a part of the small audience. What does it feel like? Could I do it? There was only one way to find out. I planned to try it out myself the very next Wednesday. So I signed up that night in advance and spent a week in front of the mirror practicing my material.

It's so funny how things pop up when you need them: I saw a notice for a stand-up comedy workshop on a public library bulletin board. I signed up for a course that very evening. About ten people showed up at the community center room, and it felt good to be a student and not the instructor for a change.

The instructors were "Poppa Nutt" and Randy "J". They were on top of their game and got right down to business.

"Ok everyone; take out your books and turn to chapter one of stand-up comedy 101. What do you mean you don't have a book? Ok, if you are in front of a laptop, open a fresh word document because the book we are using has yet to be written.

"Oh and by the way, once you have a few sentences down, don't forget to hit the save button so it isn't gone forever. Then email it to yourself so it is somewhere if your computer happens to crash. Oh no, I'm not saying it because I think you are stupid,

I'm saying it because it has happened to me more than once, including today!

"Most of you are already jotting things down all of the time when you think of it. How many of you actually fall out of bed and land on the floor trying to get to a pad of paper because some of the best material you have ever written is in your sleep? I have lost great comedy material that I have never regained. Always write it down! Even on your arm!

"Do you have a handheld voice recorder with you at all times or at the very least, a notebook? I do mean all of the time. Every time you see something that strikes you as funny, you can make fun of it and that is comedy." He held up a mini-recorder the size of a marker. "Your phone probably already has one built into it."

He was right. I just had to start using it.

"Did you see a funny sign, did you see something a person did that you find funny or crazy. Write it down, and own it! Others laugh at what they can relate to, but they may not have the ability to express it professionally or they don't have the guts to do stand-up. What you really have to ask is whether this is just a hobby you like to do, or is it what you want to do for the rest of your life. If it is the latter, then you have just made a decision to form a stand-up comedy business. Question?"

"Can't it be both?" asked a hippy dude.

"It is one or the other and you have to treat it as one or the other and not in between. Hobbies are fun and pass the time, but a business takes time, effort, and dedication to grow. They are not built overnight. You will not be an overnight sensation even if you are so good that you deserve to be. Paying the dues is a huge part and it will take some agony on your part... Some of you are thinking, 'Testify brother!' because you have already been there or will be there soon.

"Next, we are going to get ready for the stage, so if you have not been on a stage as of yet it is the type of thing that makes your insides turn to liquid so I suggest a light dinner and then eat after you perform. Those juices you are going to feel flowing, are not creative ones, they are the pee-pee squirts!

"Spotlights, cigarette smoke, a drunk trying to stare you down or pick a fight by heckling you to death—and those are the good times! Are you ready for that? I'll get into handling the heckler later, a skill you'll really need."

I was all ears. The squirts? I think there is a senior pampers special at the drugstore. Might come in handy. This is some good advice. He continued as we typed or took notes.

"You are going to hear from some of the gurus of comedy schools that you should never work free but if you don't you will never be on stage or on top of your game. If you just happen to have two nights a month that you perform for cash or drinks, and you don't do some open mic to feel out some new material and adjust it there instead of in front of a paying audience then you are in for a surprise; this time is not the squirts. It is you being canceled from your paying gig.

"Let's go ahead and back up for just a moment. Before we get on the stage and need a sheet of paper with our material on it to be able to perform, ask yourself this, 'Do I have five to seven minutes of material that I can deliver in my sleep, already memorized in my head?' If the answer is no, then you are not ready for your first squirts session quite yet."

Oh, no he mentioned squirts again. Note to self: get the large pampers!

"First, there are no formulas to follow when writing comedy material and I prefer that you do not use any. Don't get me wrong, there are rules of thumb that anyone will give to you and all differ slightly but they are good starting points. One is to have about seven minutes of material completely memorized before you get on the stage to do a five-minute gig. If you stumble on a joke, you can still get the five minutes done and done well. If you have a ten-minute gig, have fifteen minutes ready and so on.

"Two…every time you hit the stage, you need to have a voice recorder at the very least so that you remember where you did not get laughs and where you did. If possible, you need to also video tape yourself so that you can see if you were doing beginner's flaws such as looking at the floor, or pacing without acknowledging the audience."

"Sounds pretty complicated...not just telling a few jokes," said the bummed-out hippy dude.

"These are very, very important and crucial tools to have when you do self-analyses the next day. Don't ever think that you suck if it goes bad, just tweak what you did, maybe make it shorter, eliminate some and add to other lines that kept everyone making noise. You are going to have bad days but the more you get on that stage and the more you record and the harder you practice...the faster you will be a professional stand-up comedian.

"Thanks for coming to this workshop, feel free to hang-out, get some one-on-one, meet the others and exchange information. The second workshop is the boot camp.

"Stand-Up Comedy Boot Camp is simply used for lack of a better title to describe a second crucial step in your career as a professional stand-up comedian. Comedy Boot Camp is where you will need to take your career to the next level."

All of us (even hippy dude) signed up for the boot camp that Monday night, and here are the highlights of all the great advice. First off they tossed us a handout:

GET YOUR ACT TOGETHER:

- Have you finally written 15 minutes of fresh material that you will partially forget or speak too fast, thus reducing it to a 10-minute gig?
- Do you get on a stage every week at least one time, paid or not?
- Have you worked the room and spoken to every comic whether they have big tits or not?
- Do you have a resume written that expresses who you are and what you want others to know about you? There can be hints of comedy in it, but also professional wording that says you are more than a comedian. Remember, this is a business; your video is where they will see your talent.
- Did you put together a resume that lets others know that you have played at certain swinger clubs, public toilets, mud baths, or wherever you where able to stand-up on a stage and perform?
- Do you have a video that is easy to find, either on a website like this one or on a DVD? Don't link a booking agent to YouTube people. It is ok if your webpage has a video on it that goes there but you want to show initiative in having professionalism in place.

- Don't worry about the headshot unless it was with a handgun! If you don't have one you are going to have to have professional ones done regardless, even if they are from the Sheriff's Dept. I know you have a few! You look good in orange!

"Clean-up? Oh sh#t! I'm a comic not a custodian!" said one grumpy twenty-something.

"One does not exist without the other; I can promise you that!" he shot back.

"Ok, here we go with a new and improved version of what you need to do to be one step closer to where you want to be. There is no set time limit for any of these steps, but we do suggest that you stay busy all of the time so that you do not lose any of the improvements that you have made to your comedy routine.

"Listen, you are going to have to go from a trainee status to the self-management level, just below the management level. When you are ready to look for an agent or manager (very different people) to promote or manage you, they are going to want to know that there are no diapers to be changed, and if you used to think you were so great that everyone should slave for you… that thought pattern is gone!

"During the whole time that you were working your way up to breaking newbie, you needed to depend on others to be there for you, but they were there because they wanted to be. Your agent or manager (two very different roles to play) is going to be the same way. They will see something in you he or she wants to be part of. If you can, self manage in attitude and performance; he or she will take care of you while you take care of them. Your attitude will only attract those with the same attitude."

Ok then, here we go with the homework.

"Those pictures that you had your brother take of you looked good for a while, but now you are going to need some professional headshots done by a professional photographer, to put together a promotional package of yourself. You will need to have more than one type of headshot done so that you can use it for different reasons."

"You will need one that expresses you as the comic you are on the stage. This can be the class clown to dry angry humor. You will also need to have a picture you feel should be in the hands of those that create commercials or need you for a character in a sitcom. In addition, you will need a casual picture for greeting cards, follow up letters to the clubs and agents, or anyone else who should have one.

"You will also need to turn that 10 minute promotional DVD into a 20 minute DVD, solid full of funny material. This will be presented in every package you hand to every new person you want to take an interest in you. I don't care if you have to buy three beers for everyone in the club before you get on the stage and they announce that you did, make sure that you have a steady stream of laughter in that video. That will make a strong case for why you are the one they need to book! Next, post it on YouTube and pray for hits!"

"You are also going to put together a real good resume. The only way to do that is if you have thoroughly done what you should have done, you should have an impressive list that will catch the attention of whomever it needs to. Include all of the most important venues first and go from there. This should look professional, but in a way that still makes you stand out. Keep in mind, this part is the business part; the next part is the biography.

"Your CV can be witty and humorous without going overboard, but needs to be a picture of who you are. This is usually written in the third person so that it seems to be announcing you. It will also cause you to write it as if you were on the outside looking in. Make it confident so that others have confidence in you. You are a confidence man, right? Make it witty so that others find you to be funny. Make it professional so that others see you as a professional. Con man! Attention! You have graduated boot camp! Class dismissed!"

3
Getting Ready

Dinner with your parents is always a challenge.

"Are your summer classes filling up?" asked Mom, spooning out some mashed potatoes with chives.

"I'm not teaching this summer, I'm going on the road as a stand-up comedian," I said.

Silence. Dishes clanking.

"Stand-up? "said Dad." That's funny. You are not funny. You are an English professor, with tenure! Comedy? Why don't you do a poetry slam? That's more up your alley. Or write a book finally and go on tour and sell, sell, sell. It isn't dignified or academic. Now I know your getting dumped by Karen was hard…"

"Dear, don't put it that way; it was mutual," Mom said in my defense.

"No, I was dumped," I said.

"Right dumped, and now you're a comic? I don't see it." He poked at his spinach.

"You two, outside," She handed us each a beer.

This was a family tradition. Earlier it was with Pepsi, now with beer, but the idea is the same; Dad and I had to go out on the porch and talk about stuff. Like when I was caught jerking off to "I Dream of Jeannie" or when the vacuum cleaner smelled funny, or when the Catholic priest and I...well, you get the drift. It is serious man time to work out issues, my issues.

"Son, if you are thinking about becoming a comedian, then it is already obvious to me that you have the guts to do what it takes. You know, or at least you think, that you are funny enough to pull it off and that is an outstanding start. What is your game plan for this thing?" He was obviously skeptical of the whole thing. Why did I feel like I was still in high school living at home – I didn't need permission and I wasn't asking for any!

"Being a comic is a labor of love. It's a fun time, but if I want to prove my point this summer, I need to move forward, full speed. Franky and I have surfed the internet for comedy clubs with open mic nights, which we hope will lead to paying gigs later. We will head west to L.A. picking up experience and contacts, like a migrant comic. It's part dream, part vacation and who knows, it is a pretty open profession. Like

acting--one minute you are a nobody, the next a star!"
I gushed like a teenager.

"And you have every intention of coming back to the college in the fall, right?"

"Of course, unless I get a million dollar offer." I took a swig.

"Well, then enjoy, and it might even impress Karen, at the least. You know, distance makes the heart grow fonder. I don't think the last chapter has been written between you and her, so a little road trip...even with Franky...is probably a good thing."

We clinked bottles. It was nice out that evening. Summer had arrived. Stand-up Summer!

Franky thought we could raise money for my stand-up tour (really a loosely connected hodge-podge of internet surfing) by having a t-shirt party sale and kegger. He designed a rock-group style touring t-shirt listing all of my provisional stops and a flattering snapshot of me with a mic from some event a year ago. I admit it looked cool. But to be upfront, I had enough money for the tour already, even carrying Franky's extravagances. The overruling consideration was I badly needed the moral support after my break-up with Karen. Who showed up for the t-shirt party would be a big indicator of who was friend or foe. Luckily, everyone was enthusiastic and in the mood for a summer party.

It also publically forced me to commit to the tour…no backing out or skipping stops. The after-tour party was already part of the whole deal and as it later turned out, did keep me on course after a few dismal nights in dead-end clubs.

The shirts were great moral boosters even though I lost money on the idea. I see myself wearing one ten years from now. Who cares? It was a great launch! I kept a few extra shirts 'for the road'. We were deep into the keg, and I even did a short routine to an audience of friends and students who would laugh at anything. It was a great evening, but I wondered if Karen would show as promised.

I was pretty nervous answering the door that night and it got worse when Karen walked in with a gorgeous hunk of a guy right out of GQ. I felt like I had been punched in the stomach.

"Who is Karen's date?" I blustered to Franky.

"Oh him, don't you remember, he was our gay waiter at Club Rainbow's open mic night. No danger for Karen, maybe for you! Ha ha ha!"

4

On the Mic: the Basics

Our first stop was the National Satire Comedy Club open mic in nearby Fort Centertown.

National Satire was a popular magazine at one time, but now the name was attached to a franchise of comedy club/bar/disco type of place with lousy, greasy food and ugly waitresses with bad tattoos. One rumor hinted at the chain as a money laundry for Russian mobsters. Or was it the Galapagos Islands mafia? The Trilateral Commission? Daughters of the American Revolution? All of the above!

A lot of you are wondering how the comedy club thing works, so let me tell you before we hear the comics, it's actually very simple.

There are many clubs or bars in your area that do not even open on certain nights. Most of them are closed on Sunday, Monday, and Tuesday for sure and sometimes even on Wednesday I have a place here in Centerville that is closed so much that I've got a comedy night going there just because I'm sick of seeing it closed so often. I don't have the time for another project on the plate but my fellow comics help me run the show.

Let's say that you have a place that is open on Wednesday or Thursday, but those who actually show up are the town drunks and the homeless who came in to use the bathroom as a shower. You can convince the owner of that club to have an Open Mic Comedy Night so that he can gain more business. Let him know that you will take care of the details of getting a group of comics to perform, if he will provide a mic, a speaker, and a space.

Set it up a few weeks in advance, get business cards from the club, go to the open mic near your place, and advertise for about a month to all the other comedians. Chances are that they travel, just as you do, to do an open mic whenever and wherever they can. Carpooling is a great way to cement new friendships and cut drunk-driving arrests in half.

Not only will you be respected by the club owner, but you now take your turn as an Emcee. This is a great additional line on your resume. If you are good, that owner or manager will give you a couple of free meals, drinks, a few bucks and a great reference.

Let's say you do this long enough that regional amateur comedians are performing on a regular basis. Now it is time to do a venue where you will be the featured act or headliner. It can all be done, but being a professional comic takes self-management, so if you have that, then you have the ability to do this as well and have a good time.

You meet some real characters and pals among fellow aspiring comics. "Surefire" Stanley is a great example. I never knew his last name, but we all knew him. A born optimist and extrovert, he was born to do stand-up. Probably a cute goofy baby boy, he went from class clown to public speaking trophies and theater club in high school.

After seeing Richard Pryor Live, he bought a fake ID with his high school graduation money and started his real education: stand up. He is a joy to watch. He is an amazing comedian. He is the master of self-sabotage. On the one night he has the flu, a scout discovers his last-minute replacement, a now-famous comic and actor from New York. Another time he argues to fisticuffs with a major comic (over a cocktail mix!) who came out to see him perform.

Finally, he has narcolepsy and might fall asleep suddenly in a set. He tried to use that in one routine, but it backfired and he fell asleep onstage. It was funny when it happened, but he never heard the laughter. He was snoring. Tonight he was on before me. Not because he warmed up for me, but because he was awake at the moment.

"Ladies and gents, National Satire is proud to introduce the one and only SUREFIRE!" (Applause).

"Sup? I love this crowd tonight. Did you hear the one about the Nun, the Rabbi, and the rabbit? The nun was peeing in the bushes…"

"INTERNET!" screamed a young blond male heckler. Surefire ignored him.

"And the rabbit was getting soaked as the Rabbi walked by…"

"INTERNET!" screamed the same heckler, again. That was a mistake.

"The Rabbi saw the Rabbit wasn't circumcised…"

"INTERNET! INTERNET!" screamed the drunk-punk kid.

"Listen you little twink b#stard, I know you don't like it when I tell jokes about you and your family… but stop telling me INTERNET is…

Where you get your porn…

What your girlfriend uses to pick up her Craiglist tricks…

Where you posted YouTube of you fingering your dog…

And where you find cross-dressing supplies! So S.T.F.U. you pointless loser!"

Surefire boomed like an Old Testament prophet. He cut the kids to ribbons while the audience laughed their heads off. Applause and howls. He finished his set without any further heckling. You do not want to heckle Surefire. The emcee took the mic to move the evening forward.

"Tonight we have very special comic with advice on mother-in-laws, a warm welcome for the pride of India, Balle Kumar!"

He took the stage, sporting a turban and a heavy accent. It was all a part of his act.

"I wish a very good evening to all of you. Now, you can choose your husband but not your mother-in-law and that is one thing common between all types of marriage. Some women are fortunate if the mother-in-law is dead before she is married and if you are one of them, then the rest of the monologue is not meant for you. Probably you wouldn't be even present in this crowd. You would be living a life of your dreams.

"If there is anything where destiny or karma does a play a role and mostly a negative one then that is when you have a mother-in-law. Imagine a girl is playing with her favorite doll and you snatch it away and start playing with it. Will that girl ever be ok with that? Probably never! That is what you did to your mother-in-law by marrying her son. So by default a mother-in-law has to hate you and it is but natural for you to return the hatred.

"Now returning hatred by hatred is fun and that is why human beings have been indulging in it for centuries. In an ideal world a man should have had to stop talking to his mother-in-law from the day he got married or his mother-in-law should have just dropped dead with no scientific explanation or no prior medical history the minute you stepped into his life. But this world is less than ideal." [I mean either the husband or wife's mother--sadly you may have two mother-in-laws to deal with, so adjust this monologue as needed.]

"Even killing your mother-in-law is not considered as a legit act of self defense and you are charged with manslaughter. Now you have this person who is going to criticize you in everything that you do. This is that person who would constantly compare you with her herself before your husband. She will tell you the recipe for the dish that your husband likes readily but would keep out one or two vital ingredients, so that your husband feels that it's not the same. 'Mom has magic which you lack!' he will say. Even after being someone's wife she doesn't understand that the heart is not exactly a man's weakest part. Good food is not what a man always wants. She doesn't get it that a man can do without his mother but not his wife. Mom is the past and wife is the future. So on... there are many things that Mom in LAW doesn't want to understand. If you trouble her she will fall sick and extend her stay in your house, or worse, consider your house as hers. If you listen to her she will bore you to death.

"A mother-in-law is like a tail bone in the human body, it's just there. Once maybe it served some purpose but not today. I can't find a solution; the only thing I say is that one day you would be a mother-in-law too and you can harass your son's wife and get even. Maybe that's what is going on ...good night!" Applause.

The emcee signaled me to go up and take the mic. This was it. Up and at it. My pulse skyrocketed and I felt my scalp tingle in a weird way like I just did a straight shot glass of hot sauce. A weak burst of applause escorted me up the podium as the stage lights blinded me. As Billy Joel would say, the microphone smelled like a beer, and man what was I doing here? Stand-up, that's what.

Scanning the audience with an exaggerated hand to the forehead I panned slowly from left to right causing a girl I couldn't see to giggle nervously.

"Yeah...uhhhh...yeah...ok.. Just making sure no one in the audience works out or is in good shape. Uhnnn yeah, good to go. No one here is in danger of being the next Mr. Universe. Plus one is more than enough.

"A buddy of mine looks amazing! A real hunk, ask anyone, he'll tell you all about it. If he's not busy with his best friend (pause) the mirror! He'll tell everybody who will look and listen (imitating Rocky) 'Yo Adrianne! I'm ripped. I'm shredded, I'm torn up!'

"I said, 'Wow, did it really hurt that bad when you fell off your moped?'

So he tells me about his diet (imitating) 'Hey yooz I swallow six helpings of liquid protein a day.' I said, 'No need to brag, so does your average male prostitute...' No, I didn't say that cuz he'd kick my butt!

"Not that I'm jealous of his chiseled good looks, nooooo it's just that the last time I had a 6-pack I bought it at Liquor Barn. (Razz sound from audience). Well, he lifts his torn up t-shirt--really he tore it up to look like an action figure--and shows everybody his 8-pack! 8-pack? Are you kidding me? Oh yeah, he shows his abs to anyone no matter how uninterested they are! Like that pesky kid in middle school with a bad appendectomy! (I tug at my shirt) 'Look look!' Yeah, same oohs and ahhh but less jealousy and work! Just get a nasty scar and skip the gym!

"I want to help save the planet so I joined a 'green gym.' Turned out just to be painted green! Bright green. Run by a cheapskate hippy, Daffodil! The weights are just gallon milk containers duct taped to some kind of discarded pipes. Then you have to fill them with water or dirt or piss. Nice muscles! You must pump iron! Me? No, I just pump water and piss!

"Cheap! The exercise bikes are hooked up to a generator, the Stairmaster draws water for the toilet and the treadmill charges his cell phone and car battery! The solar heating and lighting is very low tech and effective: he just left the place roofless after a tornado blew it off! Free light and heat! Free rain and air! But hey, at least I can pay him in aluminum cans! Good night!" (Light applause from the crowd, obnoxious cheering from my number one fan, Franky).

I was shaking a little, but I survived my first routine with only minor jeering and a few solid laughs from a small generous audience of other amateurs and their friends. I knew my timing, material and attitude all needed work, but now I was a baptized comic at last.

Franky leaned over and whispered in my ear, "Did you squirt?"

5

The Road and Bombs Away in the West

Life on the road has many hazards, and I don't just mean Franky's driving. I'm talking about where we stayed: the White Roof Inn chain. Gas prices usually climb in the summer, so we thought we'd save a few pesos staying there. They wrote the book on cheap. It is the only place where toilet paper is thinner than a negligee! At check-in the clerk shamelessly caged for tip money and asked us how many rolls of quarters we wanted. Rolls of quarters? For what? Slot machines? In Utah?

"Never stayed here before! Ha! You'll see!" he mocked us and went back to watching TV and painting his toenails with glitter.

The towels were even thinner than the toilet paper.

And the quarters did come in handy: for soap and water in the shower, the AC, the radio, phone and TV, almost everything was coin-operated!

I walked out and stood on the tiny balcony as a small Mormon family passed by.

Just a starter family of three wives and nine overweight kids.

"Hey MIKE!" yelled Franky loud enough to stop the tribe in their tracks.

"Give me the quarters, I need to pay to open the toilet, buy paper to wipe, and another quarter to flush! HURRY! I'm dying here!" The shocked family waddled off.

Coin-operated. Make that everything.

After working several clubs, I got a little over-confident. But the gods won't be mocked.

Everybody bombs at some point.

There is no way around it. Bombing in stand-up hurts, is deeply depressing and highly necessary. My advice is to do it ASAP because the bigger they are, the harder they fall. And that means me. I bomb on my sixth routine. I had an easy baptism, a few mediocre sets with high points I built upon and stuff I cut.

By bombing I don't mean sweaty armpits, a stammering beginner's bad evening or forgetting your material and turning a polished fifteen-minute routine into an idiotic five minute rant without a dignified exit. I am talking full-blown not-funny jackass where the audience simultaneously tears into you and ignores you. Where hecklers get the laughs and you get disgusted looks or no looks at all. The audience is ashamed for you and won't make eye contact. A switchblade hurts less than the cold look in the club manager's eye as he enforces the no refund policy. Ouch.

To make it complete, be sober and not high on anything legal or illegal. That way you can't blame your unparalleled failure on anything other than your lack of ability to connect with your audience.

How shall I bomb? Let me count the ways: cockiness, overconfidence, bad horoscope. In the end I have found it is only you and the audience. You have the wrong material or they aren't there for you. I know it gets a lot more complicated than that, and each comic explains it differently, but that is how I see it.

I think I misjudged the crowd because it wasn't open mic. I was doing a free opener for a paid performer, Jeromassive, and he bought me and Franky a few drinks. Open mic crowds are different. This is a paying crowd of wolves, not lambs. They are not there to support their friend's attempt at comedy.

We passed through Mesquite, Nevada on the way to our next stop, Reno and it really caught me off-guard. I made it a great disaster by deciding to try out a new rather blasphemous piece on a secular "West Coast" crowd. They weren't offended, just bored.

"Ladies and Gentlemen, from the heartland of America, Mike Stan-thorn!" gurgled the waiter/emcee. It's S-T-A-N-T-H-O-R-P not Stanthorn, moron. Great introduction, he got my name wrong and marked me as a rube from the hills.

I walked into a glare of light and a microphone that smelled like cheap whiskey and worse.

"You should name your next child Jesus! Don't be shy, Anglos! Latinos do it, just yell,

HEY-joos! at the flea market and watch all of the vendors and half of the buyers turn around!

"Or compare it to Islam; Mohammed is the most common first name in the world!

Yell "Hey Moe!" in a bazaar! Same as the flea market, just more fleas!

"Or Jews! They aren't afraid to call a boy David, Moses, Abe. So name your kid Jesus, Anglo. But no, even the craziest white fundamentalist Christian is too chicken to name their child Jesus, even if Latinos do it! European Catholics or Greek Orthodox won't do it either.

"Imagine a Latino family--he marries her when she's pregnant with someone else's baby. But he doesn't care, and when the kid grows up, the mother demands they level with him.

'Joseph, we should tell him.' 'Hoo-kay Maria, HEY HEY-joos, come here, I am not your real father.'

"Si Papi, I know this."

"Maria and Joseph are amazed, 'How you know this, hey-joos?'

'Old story Papi I read in Bible.' See! Name your son Jesus--history comes alive!

"Rednecks! Name your Son Jesus! Man! Go to Kentucky, Tennessee, and the Carolinas; ask for Jesus at a bar! If you dare! 'Has Jesus been in tonight?' They will kneel down and start a prayer group – 'he is in our hearts tonight. Amen.' No, I mean anyone named Jesus?

Of course not! No guts! Name your child Jesus, for Christ's sake! The rednecks have every figure in the Old Testament at the bar: there's Zeke, Gabe, Mike, Jeremiah, Ben--not a single Jesus in all those Christians! Only the Latinos have the cajones to name their kids Jesus. And maybe even a few little Jesuslitas if they have too many Marys!

"Now if you are naming him Jesus, add an appropriate middle name, like 'Christ.'

Scolding the kid is now a blast: 'Jesus Christ! Clean your room! Jesus Christ! Take out the garbage! Jesus Christ stay out of your sister's underwear!'

"It won't be hard on the kid, his friends will just call him J.C. or Jaycee or Jay. Very common. Let him change his name a little, you don't want him cruci-fied, do you? Cuz kids do the funniest things!

"But the kicker is 'Kid, if you are Jesus Christ, and I am your father, what does that make me?'

The kid blurts out in shock, 'Well..it...GOD ALMIGHTY!'

"Exactly! Good night!"

The crowd was not amused, and the weight of their disapproval and near total silence (except for sneers) was a crushing weight. I was grateful the club had a backstage to hide in; I couldn't imagine a walk of shame through the mob. Surefire was snoring in the dressing room.

Sensing the mood, the emcee knew they need-ed some shock therapy, and sent in the headliner Jeromassive, the half-rapper, half comic. He really made me feel better after flopping, as he used his foul-machine-gun mouth and wiped away the memory of my pitiful performance.

"Keepin' it real is important to stand-up, and if you want street credibility, here he is, known only as Jeromassive!"

He jumped off a barstool and mounted the stage with a scowl in a black hoody.

"You're not ready to die, motherf#cker, trust me. Be ready to die any motherf#cking day don't just say it, be prepared. Plan your death before it's too late, because trust me; death actually looks for the worst possible time to take your life just to embarrass you! He does that sh#t on purpose, he's an a#sshole...He really is! Plan your death when you go out, trust me. You'll be in hell wishing you never went to the strip club that night of the shooting cause you told your girl you were working late and sh#t! The first thing you say when you get to hell is 'Sh#t, I should have never gone!'

"If you die at a strip club you know you are going to hell. Nobody in heaven will sympathize for you! Nobody in heaven will say 'Poor guy, as he placed a dollar on Coco's g-string he was shot to death.' F#ck the bullsh#t, he should be dead for being so motherf#cking cheap, goddamnit! Nobody will sympathize for you, not even your girl! She only goes to the crime scene to make sure it really was you, just in case she goes to Hell as well, you won't deny it!! Dumb motherf#cker tries to deny it in hell and sh#t 'That wasn't me, babe, I died getting struck by a truck while rescuing an orphan from an oncoming vehicle....I don't know whose body that was...'

"Dumb motherf#cker, Jesus knew it too. Jesus was just going down to hell to give you a second chance to make it into Heaven but after hearing that lie....he just turned right back, all disappointed and sh#t!

"You have to be one step ahead of being a step ahead! That's me, I got this sh#t all figured out....I thought you knew, motherf#cker! When I 'stay working late' I'll have someone text me, "Come quick! I'm in danger ......at the Strip Club." I just text back something like, 'I really shouldn't because my GF wouldn't approve but since your life is in danger I'll go rescue you...but this is an emergency...she'll understand, that's why I love her with all my heart' that way if I die that night she can read the text and think I died a hero. I had an excuse to be there...ready to die. My girl can't tell me sh#t when we get to Heaven cause she'd think I died a hero.

"You can fool her but you can't fool God....I didn't know. When she dies we'll both be in Heaven and I'm only there cause I tricked death! I thought Jesus fell for it too, to be quite honest. When we're both in Heaven God is gonna bring us together and tell us, 'You know what's interesting? You both lost your lives...heroically.... rescuing someone....at a... motherf#cking strip club!!!'

"Jesus would get ghetto on us! He'd tell us to raise the f#ck up out this bitch and leave his motherf#cking sight! He'd escort us straight to Hell personally and sh#t right on Satan's front doorstep.

"Be ready to die cause you just never know. Think about what you'll leave behind: Family, friends and neighbors. And now they would all know you had a porn collection and sh#t! F#ck the bullsh#t, don't f#ck around and die before you get rid of all that sh#t that's gonna make you look bad! Nobody feels bad about you at your funeral because they all know you had a blow-up doll under your mattress and other sh#t too! Nobody will take you seriously at your funeral! Your aunt even embarrasses you there; she's on stage f#cking up your eulogy! "I remember, HAD, (hee hee) I mean he WAS such a doll," giggling and sh#t, trying to play serious!"

"She's being a comedian at your funeral; that's why the f#ck I always said that hoe is irritating! She's up there talking about 'I'm hurt, I am...he was such a doll....it blows that he's gone. It does, it blows...he was a doll-blower; it just blew up on me when I heard, I lost my breath. It just pilled up on me, it inflated on me. He was such a doll, all I can say is it blows.'

"F#ck that bitch, but f#ck you too for not being ready to die."

His aggressive humor and foul mouth loosened up the uptight crowd. He stalked the audience from the stage like a stick-up man in a hoody, reeking of weed and danger.

"Be ready to die! If not, expect people to be giggling at your funeral! You asked for it. You were the one saying you were ready to die and death overheard your dumb#ss. Don't be the one who dies and spends all eternity wishing you would have just stayed home that night. If you are not ready to die and end up in Hell and trust me--that assh#le Satan has no remorse--he's gonna remind you of all that sh#t you left behind.

"Every time he sees you he nods and says 'Your mother was so ashamed.' That sh#t breaks your motherf#cking heart; don't f#ck around and die before you're ready cause a broken heart can't heal itself after you die. There's no coming back from death. You are nobody till somebody kills you....when someone kills you, you don't want to be that creepy somebody!

"I'm not saying don't own anything you shouldn't have, own it. Just be one step ahead of step ahead and you'll be good. That's why the f#ck I label my sh#t. I put post-it's on it that say 'Confiscated from little orphan boy, James!' That's why I'm going to Hell! Motherf#cking orphans done ruined my resume to Jesus, goddamn it! But I label my sh#t so when I die, I die a role model and with some honor and sh#t! Be ready to die. I am! Everything I own that I shouldn't own has some sort of explanation on it 'cause where I'm from, you just never know."

He was over his allotted time limit, a real no-no, but he was on a roll, and who was going to dare to cut him off? Let it roll!

"You can leave a half rolled joint in your room to answer the front door and BAM! A motherf#cking stick up! You got shot for answering the door at the wrong time. You weren't even the target! The dumb#ss fiends got the wrong address! Joker always f#cks up his sixes and nines...you just never know!

"I have a diary I write in, just to explain why I have the things I have. My last entry says:

'Dear Diary, as I skipped to Church, as usual I ran into Toby.....yes, Toby, the Orphan. Toby had a container with marijuana and told me he wanted to try it for the first time but was scared to try it alone. He was asking me to join him....Diary, you know me better. I refused and talked him into giving me the container because he shouldn't be smoking that garbage. I took it home and I was gonna flush it but then I thought ...You know, wouldn't it be swell if HE flushed it? That way he knows what he's doing is the right thing I'm saving the container until he comes over next week to flush it together. I'm proud of Toby, Diary....Damn Proud!'

"F#ck the bullsh#t, when I say I'm ready to die....I'm ready to die! I don't just say that sh#t, I really do this sh#t! My plan is foolproof. The only ones who will be mad at me at my funeral are the Orphans, and they're not going where I'm going. I'm going to Hell because of them! At least I thought so! I was wondering why I saw a few orphans answering to Satan; Jesus wasn't too bright cause he remembered I fooled him... he forgot and I framed the Orphans!"

He walked off the stage, ignoring the applause. Jeromassive didn't bomb, he dropped the bomb!

The night ended with a much tamer comic, Joe English:

"I'm not going to go that far and say that secondhand pornography can kill you, like secondhand smoking certainly can, but it sure can do some pretty excessive damage to your internal organs, brain specifically. The problem with secondhand pornography is that it is almost impossible to avoid.

Let's face it, it's all around us. Ever since the wireless internet made its debut, we've been exposed to waves of websites traveling from wireless routers to a huge net of commercial and personal computers. And let's be honest, a lot of those websites are just here to satisfy our sexual desires.

"Signals carrying videos of naked girls doing all kinds of good and not-that-good things are traveling through our bodies all the time. And our brains register it. Remember those old statistics that said an average male adult thinks about sex every twenty seconds. Well, you can say goodbye to those. An average male today thinks about sex every second, even when he's sleeping, eating or crying.

"Every time our neighbors decide to look at porn, our brain is there to register it. We're not even aware of it. And not all categories of porn are all that good.

Today you've got porn with horse involved, you've got them without horse, you name it. Scary shit. All that crap is being poured on our brain constantly so that sooner or later we will start feeling the effects.

"You want proof? Let's go back twenty years or so, when I was a teenager. I was as horny as they come. I remember I would walk to school for a mile or two; it was dark, right before the dawn. I had to pass by a city park and a cemetery, but I was not afraid. You know why? Because I had just found out about sex! If I heard leaves rustling, or bushes moving I wasn't running. I would have instant boner instead. The part of my brain was telling me, 'Hey, maybe it's a naked girl coming your way.'

"Not likely, but hey, you never know. Good old times. Let's see if today's youngsters can do that. Still not convinced? Give it another twenty years or so. Pretty soon you'll have three categories of sexual orientation: straight, gay and sexually inactive. You'll have people who will just say, 'I've had enough of it. I'm sick of thinking about it, I'm sick of doing it, just leave me alone.' But by then it will already be too late to go back to normal. If indeed, what we had can actually be called normal. G'night!"

6
After Bombing a Roast

I was a little gun shy after bombing and needed some advice from the resident philosopher, not so much a bucket from the fountain of wisdom, but rather a "squirt" from Franky. He cleared his throat the way professors do when they are about to launch into a long, long speech (rant).

"Ugrgrrgggggg...hmmm...hhggghh...You know Michael this is another required experience. Can any comic, great or small, ever hope to have a bomb-free career? Did the great tree of comedy, the immortal Lenny Spruce, not bomb?"

"Lenny Bruce," I corrected him.

"Same-same! Suck it up big boy! Cross it off your stand-up summer must-do list. Bombed. Check.

Knock-em-dead. Check! Getting stiffed on a comp! Check! Getting paid! Laid! Check! Check! Getting discovered, getting on TV! Yes!" His goofy face and confidence in my ability cheered me up.

"I feel better already."

"You should! Just getting closer to the big show. Hey, you need a mantra, private prayer to say before every set... because not even the gods can improve your jokes!"

"What does that mean?"

"Take it both ways!" he said with a foolish grin.

Franky was right so I thought about it and composed a mantra:

Who wants to laugh? – They do.

Who can make them laugh? I can.

Who will make them laugh? – I will.

To put it all behind me, I was invited to a comedy roast; luckily I wasn't the feature!

One of my favorite clubs, in my limited experience, is Capt. B's Master Bait Comedy Club. The semi-retired sea-charter captain is generous with drinks while other clubs require you to bring at least four drink-buying fans to the open mic. He might spot you a drink and demand to be paid with a set or just one really funny, dirty joke he hasn't heard. A joke he hasn't heard? It took me ten tries, and I was lucky!

The club is always packed and 'The Cap' has

major contacts with big name comics. Anyway, tonight was a roast of the mariner with a funny bone, and new friends and old ones jumped in to help. Here are a few of the zingers he took:

He sticks to the old values: life, liberty, and the pursuit of… fat chicks!

On women: This guy is so open-minded, he now has three eyebrows! Ahoy!

I heard the Captain lost his Speedo trunks while swimming at the beach. Several people tried to retrieve them, but they were eaten by a shrimp.

I hear the Cap is Italian on "her" fairy godmother's side. Or is it hairy-fairy muther? He is so bi-polar he lives in a split-level house. The bathtub has a waterfall. Flowing up from the toilet on the ground floor to the roof! Man the poop deck!

Talk about a slacker. Captain's got a snooze button on his smoke alarm.

The reason we subject the Cap to a roast is because stoning is illegal. And we tried, but Pakistan was booked!

The Cap has no shame. He once complimented the Queen on her lack of panty lines and asked who ironed her knickers. She disliked his cigarette and asked him if he would please not "smoke fags" in front of her – he insisted he never killed anyone, regardless of sexual orientation!

He's suing the state because on his girlfriend's driver's license, they gave her an "F" in "Sex." He thought she had worked hard with him and deserved an "A"!

I was going to call on our guest of honor now, but he's not quite finished with MY dessert yet. 'Thar she blows!

At the roast, an old girlfriend of the Captain brought the local telephone book with a new cover and said it was his little black book listing all the women he had...and then it fell over sideways because it was so heavy.

People were on the floor laughing, including me! He loved it.

Done correctly a roast can be a fun way to "honor" someone. They can be funny and are unforgettable when done well. But there are some dos and don'ts when having a roast. So I emailed a few comics experts some questions.

Q: First of all, who is a good candidate for a roast besides cannibals?

A: Whether it's a birthday surprise, a retirement party or for some other occasion where there is one person being honored, a roast is perfect (as long as your guest of honor has a sense of humor!). It's probably a good idea to check with them first to make sure they'll be comfortable on stage. Then proceed to make them VERY uncomfortable!

Q: *Do all the "roasts" and "toasts" have to be negative? Even if they do deserve it, badly!?*

A: Absolutely not. Only the good ones! But it seems like roasts (and toasts, too) are funnier when they insult the person. If you remember, Dean Martin and Don Rickles used to host the Friar's Club roasts (or whatever it was called). They were televised, and all of the celebrities got up, one by one, and made fun of whoever was the night's honoree. So, as long as the negative comments are not hurtful and are in good fun...anything goes.

Q: *How many people do you need to make it a fun event? I guess it takes at least two...*

Well, roasting someone at the dinner table probably doesn't qualify as a real, true roast. I remember that on my 35th birthday, my friends roasted me. As I recall, there were probably 40 to 60 people in the room. The worst teasing came from my brother, of all people, who let the crowd know that my mother liked him best. The more people in the room, the more ruckuses there are. The more people who present, the more fun it is.

Q: *Is anything really off limits? Like their Swiss bank accounts and sex toys?*

A: Not really, if you have good life insurance... Obviously, you don't want to bring up past relationships that are still lingering, or talk about how many women a man has dated...if he's there with someone new. You have to use common nonsense, and remember this is about being humorous--all in good fun. Like how you and your secret pals used to pants-down spank each other with a spiked board; just normal, good clean fun.

It was a fun roast, and the Captain's face was red with laughter, alcohol and the sheer joy of basking in the glow of attention from the comics who cherished him and his club. We all slammed a round of drinks (on his own tab!) in his honor and departed into the night, exiting the comedy club, sucking into our lungs the smell of cigar smoke, sweat and laughter that makes your belly hurt.

7

Good Advice for the Road

The time passed quickly with Franky, and the shows became less frightening. I think this was because we got into a routine as soon as we hit a new town, and a routine not only speeds up time and adds a familiar touch to a 'foreign' town, but the homogeneity of the American Midwest towns adds a reassuring tone to the trip.

We'd hit town, cruise the main street, find the club and check in at a decent motel. Then our first real meal of the day, a late afternoon hamburger and beer at a greasy spoon diner.

The second meal of the day, happy hour, followed. A short nap or walk before the show, and the night had begun. It was a nocturnal existence, a comedy swing or graveyard shift, depending on the day of the week. I always looked forward to talking or texting Karen with the latest news, now a daily event. Franky haunted bookstores and thrift shops.

I emailed Poppa Nutt and Randy "J" from Starbucks about a few issues related to road life. They graciously replied and wrote that I owed them lunch, my first-born child and a free copy of my future CD for their online comments:

"I am going to touch on a couple of issues when it comes to comic etiquette. The first one is involving other comedians that will be performing with you that evening. I'm sure that if you ever had a parent, grandparent, or someone else that taught you right from wrong in your life, then you have heard the term, "Do unto others as you would want done unto you."

I'm not going to get into a 3-page list of what that means because it speaks for itself. Nevertheless, far be it from me not to add a couple at the very least.

"First…

Whether you are at an open mic or at a comedy club and your allotted time is five, ten, fifteen, or thirty minutes, then that is your time, not more and not less. How will you know without a watch? Clubs will give you the light (We will go over that on another page) or you will have a clock on the stage hidden behind a speaker that you can see. The same goes for an open mic.

I'm going to say that you are going to be allowed a grace period of about thirty seconds on either side of the clock. If I was you, though…I would make it on the lesser side than the, "I ran over my time" side.

I thought about Jeromassive as I sipped my coffee, reading eagerly.

If you go over your time then you are stealing time from the person that is up next, but if you go under then that will leave you time to welcome the host back to the stage where he will, in return, tell the audience to give you a nice big round of applause."

"Next…

Unless you are the "Headliner" then what's your hurry? Stick around for a bit to support the next comedian. Oh, you don't know him or her; you don't like anyone else's material but your own? Good luck on making it in this business then. That person may have been your ticket to the big show at some point and they have a good memory.

How about telling them, "Nice set" even if you didn't feel it was funny. How many comedians do you see on the TV all of the time that are actually not funny? I see a whole lot that I can't believe are up there but they paid their dues and had enough recognition to sell the show. Strangely, a lot of 'funny people' don't seem funny to you, and yet to the right crowd on the right night, they crack-up an entire club. Same with you!"

The coffee hit me as I read, confirming much of what I had seen on the road.

"Keep in mind that the "Emcee" is also a comedian and can introduce you with the same respect as you give to him or her. When you are going on to the stage you say, "Give it up for the emcee," and when you come off the stage, "Give it up again for your emcee." In return, he says the same for you and there is no dead time that you need to fill.

Do unto other comedians as you want done unto you. If that doesn't sound simple enough, then good luck at your other job; you are going to need it. Whether you are at an open mic or at a comedy club and your allotted time is five, ten, fifteen, or 30 minutes, then that is your time, not more and not less. How will you know without a watch? Clubs will give you the light or you will have a clock on the stage hidden behind a speaker that you can see. The same goes for an open mic.

See how that sounded exactly the same? That's because I copied and pasted it. First, believe it in your heart and keep it there forever that, as far as the club is concerned, open mic does not need to exist and you do not need to perform. In other words, they are doing you the favor and not the other way around. Therefore, you need to follow the rules.

You need to be smart enough to know how to time your skit during rehearsal. You are better off thirty seconds under (No more) than going thirty seconds over, I assure you, if you get the light at a comedy club, it means, "Get the f#ck off the stage NOW!" You have worn out your grace period and you are breaking into another person's set. If that other person is you, then how will you finish your set without enough time? If it is another person that you managed to screw, then you just burned a bridge with a person that may have been able to help you in the future.

In a comedy club, there are two shows a night on Friday and Saturday with thirty minutes to clear the room and make it new again for the next crowd to come in and enjoy the show. If you are the reason they have less time to get that done, then you have just pissed off the host, manager, and the waitresses that are trying to tab out and clean up. You are going to have to hope that you are not too prideful to march your butt up to the club team and make a formal apology or you may be doing your shows in another town before too long.

These people can make you or break you in the world of comedy. You need to treat each one of them as if they are the CEO of a company that you want to work for forever...because they are. Once they feel that they are no longer in need of your services, it's off to another city to start over again. Life is hard enough without making it harder on yourself and you do so by making it harder on others. A little bit of pure comedian etiquette will go a long way.

Do your individual thing; tell jokes in regards to what you like, what you're excited about, and incidents in your lifetime. People will love what you do when you love that which you do too, and you'll even make more friends. Of course not everybody is likely to adore you, but hey, that's just how life is.

Mike, you are a naturally funny person, obviously you are already in front of the ones that aren't. That's good, since it will likely be much easier for you than it will for somebody who's not. However, when you get used to it, you'll have the ability to perform effortlessly since you used step by step comedy to achieve success."

I wished they were on tour with me. My eyes scanned the computer screen.

"Next you'll wish to start studying and learning all you can. Absorb just as much regarding the subject as you possibly can. Knowledge is a key advantage. The more you have, the more opportunities open for *you. Take the time to watch a couple of videos of your favorite stand up comics performing their routines and take in exactly what they're doing. Watch and understand how they tell their jokes, move about the stage and connect to the target audience.*

Read as much as you are able to about comedy, every facet of it, from telling jokes, to writing them, to performing them. You need to be the greatest, so do exactly what it will take to be the very best comedian. After you've got a good knowledge base go and do something, but keep learning along the way. After you've taken action yourself, jot down notes to make up your own funny stories, take note of how you intend to act them out on stage and just how you're likely to cope with the audience and so forth. The last stage of step by step comedy is to locate a place to try out your act. Try it on your friends, family, co-workers, people in the pub, etc. If everything goes well you can progress up the ladder and start visiting different events like birthday celebrations and school gatherings like reunions. You are already doing this.

You'll know if you're carrying out a good job because people will laugh at the act. Not only can they laugh, but they also may come up to you and discuss exactly what a good job you're doing. If you've managed to make it this far and you want to proceed further go ahead, then take your time and use these stand up comedy tips to help you reach your goal. Hang in there, Mike--go the distance. –Poppa and Rand

Their advice was valuable, and things were looking up. Club owners were calling each other and I was on the radar as an early crowd guy and non-smoking show. I had decided early on not to do bathroom humor or lots of foul language. I like it when others do it, but it's not me. I was developing a mini-reputation as being easy to work with, on time and not fussy.

Rather quickly a free drink became a free meal and then it happened, in Montana: I got paid out of the blue. A club manager stuffed a $20 bill in my shirt and tore up my dinner bill (which included Franky's steak). I glowed with the joy of recognition. Still, was this it? It was bittersweet, but it wasn't the Holy Grail I was after.

Looking back on the week, I logged off and opened my diary to end the evening:

Dear Diary   Someday in July

What does a mic smell like? Booze and fear. Less fear now, fewer butterflies and yet I am too busy trying to keep my act tight and funny. Not good. I need to relax more and enjoy the other comics. I am too serious and clean. Some are calling me "diz" for Disney (term for a clean comic) but at least when I'm up there, it's me. My timing is better, and I'm learning.

This Wednesday when the crowd went on a laughing jag at one of my jokes, I let it roll, and raised my eyebrows to milk it. Last week I would have raced to the next joke. But why push it? If the idea is to get laughs, let them laugh, which is the whole frigging point!

On the other hand, I miss Karen so much I want to call this whole thing off and drive straight home. I hear it in her voice--she misses me. Who am I kidding? I'm not a stand-up comedian; I'm a hack English professor. Where did I get this idea, out of a desperate need to laugh? And if only that little man with a hammer would stop hitting me on the head. Screw this whole scene. I am hung over, undersexed, bored of clubs and ready to strangle Franky. But hell no, I won't give up because I don't know how to quit. I'm only able to finish what I start, the old Stanthrop pigheadedness. I may go down in flames, fail in action. But I will fulfill my tour t-shirt no matter how louse-infested the hotel, skanky the barmaids in the urine-soaked dive bars, no matter how I bomb or am heckled by a crowd of drunk losers, I will give it right back. God, it will be so easy to go back to teaching this fall. So easy. I hate you, stand-up summer!!!

We do it again tomorrow nite, yours, Cognacman

8
Scouted

Despite my diary rants, I am usually very upbeat and interested in doing a better job on the stage. I also tried to get into clubs where my million-to-one chance of getting spotted was better. I didn't have the luxury of time so I was overworking myself with several shows a night. So much for a vacation! I also needed to know more about cutting deals and finding an agent.

I remember Poppa Nutt and Randy "J" telling me that a booking agent is a very different person than your manager. In some cases, they may be partially the same, but not when you are doing more than three nights a week. You will have issues at some point, if you do not have both parties on your team, working as one solid unit.

Even though they will "want" to do what's best for

you, a real entertainment manager will actually have the ability to accomplish it, due to his or her connections in the field. If you want to hire a friend later to take care of other things, then that is great if the $$$ is there. A real manager will also look out for your best interests; just find the one that fits you. I did the easiest thing, I just appointed Franky. He owes me money so I don't have to pay him anything. He was happy to surf the net and generate leads to clubs and play sidekick.

You could do your own managing and save about 15% of your income. This will more than likely be the only option that you have at first. Your booking agent will guide you in some direction and may even give you a name—a person he or she believes you should work with when the time is right. If the agent is good and you trust them, then they probably work well with that manager and it will be a win-win for the both of you.

When will you know the time is right? According to my coaches, you will be so busy that you start to forget things on the calendar. You don't even know what state you are in anymore and you haven't written new material in two months due to your managing the workload. This can cause many serious issues for you, including your career. Some of the duties that you are dealing with on a day-to-day basis are the ones that your manager will need to take off your mind. I remember them saying that those were a few of the basics.

I fished around in my backpack for a handout they had on agents. I found it:

Rules for Miss Managers

- Negotiate with the agent about your tour
- Make sure your tour dates don't overlap each other
- Make sure your drug dealer, bookie and loan shark are paid on time
- Make sure your hotel arrangements are secure (hookers)
- Handle all of the marketing of yourself
- Arrange photo shoots
- Contact the local 'what's going on' tabloids and webpages to let them know where you will be playing
- Prepare your auditions and presentations
- Make sure that you are moving ahead and not falling behind
- Remember what city you are in
- Proof read ALL of your material
- Wear dark-colored anti-squirt pants with thick underwear

This is a small list, so if things are moving along, you will certainly need a manager, don't you think?

The Booking Agent is a different story and can be summed up in a brief sentence. They make sure that you have paying gigs that you need to show up to and make sure they are the best ones available for you at that time in your career, so that everyone makes the most $$$ that can be made. They get between 10-15% of the negotiated purse.

Well, enough of that, time for an update party with myself:

Dear Diary   Some damn day in late July

I love LA. Gotta love LA. I actually hate LA. But I am in a better mood after talking to Karen just now, and my act is hitting its stride in the West Coast clubs where the pay varies from free drinks and a meal to $50 cash or the offer of illegal and semi-legal refreshments. My material is tested and my timing is on the dime. All fear is gone, and I went up last night and took the mic and stared at the audience with a look that started them laughing without saying anything. That was a major breakthrough. Yes.

I think a lot of Midwestern wannabe comics like me agree LA is one of several holy pilgrimage sites for stand-up comedy. NYC, Boston, LA and South Beach...but the last one is about chicks, not comedy. But LA is where it is happening for me; and, baby, let it happen! I am funny, I am tanned and in cool threads, a far cry from the uptight English professor in my other life. Can I go back? Yes, I will go back, simply because I am going broke on this working vacation. There is no money in this profession unless you are at the tippity-top. And that isn't gonna happen in the few remaining weeks. I am having a great time, but I am still too heartbroken to chase anything but the ego rush of applause and the stories and advice of stand-up veterans. The stories are endless!

Franky saw a real doctor and got a California Medical Marijuana Card. He is "healing" non-stop, but at least I don't have to worry about him getting arrested. Or even about him getting out of bed. He hooked up with a redhead with a few inches of her body not tattooed, and he entertains her with philosophy. She reciprocates by teaching him tantric yoga. Pizza delivery and a midnight naked swim in the hotel pool fill out their busy day of activities. That's our stand-up summer routine, which will soon end.

Goodnight, dear diary, yours as always, Cognacman.

I became a nocturnal animal, napping in my room or at the pool all day, arising at sunset to hit the comedy clubs, sometimes four shows a night into the wee hours. I had settled with the idea that this was how it would end. It was nearly the end of July and we were running out of time and money. The t-shirt comedy stops were all made, and after a few more shows we would head home and get ready for the coming semester.

Boy, was I wrong.

After a well-executed but normal set, an executive-type I had seen before walked up to me.

"David Fieldstein, the Comedy Channel." We shook hands in the traditional way, even though I often saw him bump fists with trendy comics. I was to find out why. I was to be his conservative dunce.

"My pleasure…" I said as he crushed every bone in my hand.

"Call me Dave. I liked your set last week at the Costa Mesa Comedy Dive and asked about you. I came in extra tonight and was again impressed." He was looking not at me, but at a pair of blondes at the bar.

"Thanks Dave, that means a lot to me. There is a lot of talent here tonight."

"True. Have you heard of our program Hump day Humor?"

"Sure, Comedy Channel, Wednesdays at nine p.m." I remembered that from ads, I never really watch it, but now was not the time to offer that information.

"The format is an intro piece from a new, rising comic before the headliner comes on, the more established comic, the one we really want to showcase. I have you in mind for an intro piece, so what do you say to a shot on national cable?"

"I say two things. 'Hell, yes and why me?'" I was like a wide-eyed deer in the headlights.

"Mike, I shoot straight. I like Surefire better. I like Jeromassive better than you. I just can't use Jero with his dropping the f-bomb every second word. I have tried to work with him, clean up his material. In a club, no one cares about swearing, but we can't have bleep, bleep, bleep every other word from an intro act. It does not work for the home audience. It is bad enough all the bleeps for the headliner. Your role is this: you come on squeaky clean and are funny enough to warm up the audience, but not funny enough to upstage the main act. The headliner will be better than you, must be better than you. Your material is clean; you are not a flake or a druggie. I can't count on Surefire. Love his style, but he does not come through in a tough spot, he sleeps under pressure and the camera does not love him. That's it."

"Count me in," I stammered.

"Give me a solid five minute Disney-clean routine, solid delivery, solid timing. It pays five hundred dollars. No more. We have total rights over the tape and material. You got an agent? Manager?"

"Franky Ledbetter," I deadpanned, hoping to cut him in on the action.

"Never heard of him. Here's my card. Don't call me. Call this one, my assistant, Sara.

We tape Wednesday at four p.m. to a live, but tame audience and some professional laughter. No hecklers. Sara will give you all the details. Nice working with you, Mike."

He slapped my back and walked off in a beeline to the blondes at the bar, leaving the scent of cologne I can't afford. A real smooth operator. I forgot to thank him for all the left-handed compliments of being good enough to fluff for a pro. But that is where and what I am at this point, he just saw me and called me as I am.

Then it hit me: national cable TV and $100 a minute to do stand-up. It had all been worth it. I choked up and my eyes watered involuntarily. I looked at the floor, afraid of who might see me almost crying and just enjoying the moment. My stand-up summer was a success by my low standards; I had done it, no matter what else happened. I am going national.

I felt happy, very lucky and extremely guilty. I had managed to leapfrog over those who had really paid their dues. I hope they wouldn't turn on me. I vowed to help them if this led me anywhere. It is what it is. Show biz.

9
TV Taping

When we went in for the taping I was more nervous that a sheep in a camp full of horny Australians. Franky took a break from the redhead to accompany me and play agent.

The studio was amazing. So much technology, so much money. The $500 they offered me may have barely paid for the crew's daily coffee. But this was about proving I had made it doing stand-up comedy and nothing else. Being on a national cable show would make me a winner in Karen's eyes. Oh, her voice on the phone when I told her about it!

Then something on the left caught my eye.

"Franky! Is that Doug Stanhope over there, walking out?"

"Yeah! It is. He rocks. Maybe he'll be back and we

can score a free CD from him!"

"Do you think I'm opening for him? They never told me who the headliner would be. I was so amazed by the offer it slipped my mind to ask."

"Really? I know who it is, I asked Sara yesterday," he said, goofily looking around.

"Well, who is it?"

"Oh, no, you'd just be…go on, guess!"

"Franky, who is it? Come on." I was already nervous without his silly guessing game.

"No, three guesses!" he teased.

I know Franky well-enough to shoot out three rapid fire guesses or I will just prolong my misery.

"OK, Doug Stanhope, Pauley Shore or Chris Rock."

Franky fell against a lighting prop laughing loudly. "YOU open for Chris Rock!!?? Hahahahahahahha! You! Hahahahha that's good! HEY EVERYBODY! He thinks he's opening for Chris Rock! Really! He just told me that!"

"No I didn't, Franky, stop attracting attention."

Three bored stagehands with silly smiles walked over.

"You? No, you ain't opening for Chris Rock. Get off the pipe, man!"

"He also said he's opening for Pauley Shore!" shouted Franky, loud enough for Ohio to hear.

"Sheezzz," said the other, looking me up and down in disgust.

"I did not…" I tried to explain.

"Or Doug Stanhope!" Franky felt impelled to chime in.

"No dude, he just left," said the taller one.

This intelligent exchange ended when David strolled over out of nowhere and broke up the chatter, directing me over to make-up and before I knew it, I was hustled on a stage in front of the paid audience, taped and sent home. Boom! Bang! In the can and out the door. I did it in one take. David said 'good enough' and handed me an envelope. The next comic already took the stage for his five minutes. Assembly line. That was it.

"We will air it on Wednesday in three weeks." He smiled with empty eyes and walked off in a cloud of cologne worth more than gold, with his assistant Sara and two others in tow. Not even a goodbye. Mr. Charm himself. I opened the envelope and found a check for $500.00 and "filler AV 5mn" in the memo line. Filler audio visual five minutes, that's me!

Back at the hotel bar, stinging from aftershock, I slugged down two large cognacs and tried to cope with what just happened. Too much had taken place too fast. I felt slightly violated at the swift treatment I was given, but what can you expect from a guy like

David? I turned to Franky who was "sexting" his red-head and polishing off a Heineken.

"Franky, you never did tell me who I'm opening for, who is it?" I asked, still ruffled.

"I forgot. Some woman. Susan? No. Sally? Shirley! Or Samantha…" his stoned brain struggled with short-term memory loss. "Sara, Seeopatra, Simba, Shakara, Seatoad…" he sing-songed like a three-year-old.

"Franky?"

"Yes?"

"Shut the hell up. Cheers."

Clink. We had done it. Who cares who the head-liner is, really?

Looking back at the taping, a great thing about stand up comedy is that it's pretty damn easy to record on film, and a good recording crew can get the essence of the performance across. Here's what I remember from the guys at the station.

The traditional way to record a comedy performance is either to run a line from the line-out of the PA straight into a digital recorder (or computer, or whatever). This poses a problem if you have a low quality microphone. The mic's limitations will show up on the recording, so never use a cheap mic. You can run it through an amplifier later and mic the amp if you're looking to get a more natural, in-the-audience sound. You can also mic the speakers live, but I think it's best to have the original signal. It gives you more options later on, in the remix.

It's a good idea to use a large diaphragm condenser microphone at the back of a room to record the crowd sound. Otherwise it can sound like the comedian is dying when he's not. You can up the volume of the crowd mic, alternately, to make the comedian sound like he's getting more laughs--there's nothing wrong with this kind of "sweetening" if it results in a better product. Just don't be super obvious or it backfires and makes you look like a fake with canned TV sit-com laughs.

When mixing any type of stand up comedy, you're usually going to want to add a lot of compression, unless the signal from the PA already compressed the vocals quite a bit. Many stand-up comedians use their tone and volume to accent jokes, and while that's great live, it can be difficult to deal with on a recording, especially when going from quiet to loud; if people have to repeatedly mess with their stereos to get the volume right, they probably just won't listen to the stand up CD. In summary, leave it to the pros if you want a quality product.

With that being said, remember, if it sounds good, it's fine, regardless of what rules it breaks. What the hell! Comedy Channel cable equals victory! Declare victory and retreat! Home and sweet Karen, here we come! Goodbye L.A. You were a great audience!

10
Stand-up or Fall

Despite how we both mock Centerville, both Franky and I counted the last few miles home. As the territory became more familiar, we became chatty and visibly excited: it is nice to come home. And everyone was waiting for us at my parent's house, even Karen.

She walked up like a lovely vision. "Hi big shot. Nice you could stop by. I am so proud of you!" And planted a big kiss on my lips and held me tightly. I was a returning hero of sorts, I had found the beginner's Holy Grail of Comedy and that Wednesday night I would be unleashed for my five (not fifteen) minutes of fame.

Wednesday night the crowded house sat glued to the newly purchased big-screen TV. The house over-flowed with students, faculty, family and Karen in my arms again. Heaven.

Intro to show blurb, then came my routine. No, not yet, wait, a rug cleaning commercial.

OK, now! No, a roach trap commercial with an ex-congressman as the roach.

Now the headliner, Ms.Santini the transvestite, non-funny comic.

What happened? Did I get my dates wrong? Where was my piece?

Everyone was flabbergasted, silent, confused, and aghast.

My cell rang. It was Sara.

"Hi Mike. Listen, this happens all the time. Two last minute ads were sold at a discount and took your spot. Plus the headliner was a bit long. It doesn't mean we won't use it at some point as filler. David is waving at me, gotta go. Talk later. Bye."

So that's how it works. Franky began ranting. Everyone was understanding and sympathetic and a little dazed.

"There's always next summer," I told everyone after explaining. Karen hugged me. We were back together, show or not. That's what mattered most of all.

As an epilogue, Dave called me two weeks later. I was already into the swing of fall classes and my well-worn academic rut. I saw his number on the telephone screen so I did something I never do. I answered my phone, mostly because I had heard several reports of the clip being shown on TV at odd hours of the day, but I never saw it.

"David?"

"No, its Sara, he's on another line, how have you been?

"Great, Sara! Nice to talk to you..."

"Hey Mike, to update you, your clip has been shown as filler and to cover dead air space over seventeen times. And we didn't have negative responses. I bet that makes you happy! Of course, because we own all rights and don't pay you anything, we could use it a thousand times. Isn't that great?! Think of the exposure."

"Yes, Sara, I love exposing myself to the public, especially for free."

"Great Mike, I'm transferring now, bye!"

"Bye!"

"Dave here, Mike! Your clip is a great hole-stopper. We used it lots of times, and almost used it several more, but cut it for a paid commercial or promo deal. Anyway, it's not about the quality of your performance, it was who saw it and liked it. It was shown to the Comedy Channel senior citizen focus group and they found you were not terrible, not too boring and classified you as a show they would watch while doing something else. Just what advertisers want! I told our executives you have a ninety minute pilot ready to be taped. After just a few days of indecision and two better comedians that turned us down, you came in under budget as a desirable last resort. But hey, $9,000 for 90 minutes is what we got for you. We tape in Hollywood Sept. 15."

"Dave...I can't just leave, I am in the middle of the semester. How long would we tape? I could work something out."

"Listen Mike, in or out? The pilot taping is open-ended. It involves skits, live action with a studio audience, guest comics, special effects, make-up, producer, 90 minutes is a two-hour show with commercials thrown in. We need total commitment on your end from now to the end of the year, maybe less. I can't and won't say. Again, be straight with me, what is your decision?"

I knew this was it. A test of my personal loyalty. Was I an English professor or a stand-up comic? It wasn't a pretty choice to make, but it was a pretty easy choice to make.

"My teaching takes priority," I said firmly, as my heart crumbled.

Silence.

Then he spoke.

"Then we come to you."

"Centerville?" I choked.

"Yeah, I know just the crew to send to do it as punishment. Uh, for them, that is. They are fresh out of detox and rehab, or were, they had a small slip, a week-long bender in Jamaica. The rum, girls and weed worked on them, and by the time I sent my enforcer to load them up, they were shooting a porn film on my dime! They are currently grinding out a commercial for one of our sponsors in the blazing heat of Arizona under watch, so they will be happy to get out of there and work in boring Centerville where nothing happens! Like an upgrade to a half-way house! Did anything good ever come out of that hick town of yours? Done deal, Sara will call you!"

Called ended. Then just as suddenly my cell rang.

"Hi Sara. Stand-up this fall?"

"Hi Mike, stand-up or fall!" she teased. Yeah, I thought, let's do this.

So that is my story. I sit here in the dark comedy club after the Wednesday evening open microphone, knowing I need to get some sleep. I have classes to-morrow, and the Comedy Channel crew arrives on Friday. I don't know how the next crazy chapter of my stand-up saga will work out, but I will always have the stand-up summer. Give your dreams a chance. The future is unwritten. See you in the funny parlors.

The End

<u>Special thanks to</u>:

Poppa Nutt and Randy "J", Jeromassive, Surefire, Jeremy Alvarez, Xiaoqi Li, Balle Kumar, Joe English, Doug Stanhope, icomedy.com and stand-up comedy.com

CPSIA information can be obtained at www.ICGtesting.com
Printed in the USA
LVOW08s0115140816

500307LV00001B/5/P